Clarion Books
a Houghton Mifflin Company imprint
215 Park Avenue South, New York, NY 10003
Copyright © 2002 by Daniel J. Mahoney

The text was set in 16-point Schneidler Roman.
The illustrations were executed in watercolor.

www.houghtonmifflinbooks.com

Printed in Singapore.

Library of Congress Cataloging-in-Publication Data

Mahoney, Daniel J., 1969-
The Saturday escape / by Daniel J. Mahoney.
p. cm.
Summary: Three friends feel guilty about going to story hour at the library
instead of doing what their parents told them to do.
ISBN: 0-618-13326-7
[1. Behavior—Fiction. 2. Responsibility—Fiction. 3. Animals—Fiction.] I. Title.
PZ7.M27685 Sat 2002
[E]—dc21   2001032430

TWP 10 9 8 7 6 5 4 3 2 1

The Saturday escape

escape

Daniel J. Mahoney

Clarion Books New York

for Jean

It was Saturday, Jack's favorite day– story hour day! At 9:30 sharp, he zipped down the stairs and headed for the door.

"Hold it right there, young man," growled his mother.
"No story hour for you until you pick up your room."

Moments later, Jack emerged from his bedroom. "All done!" he called. Then he dashed outside.

8

Jack ran all the way to Angie's house. "Are you ready for story hour?" he asked her.

"I can't go," said Angie. "I have to practice piano."

"Wait," said Jack. "I have an idea. All you have to do is play the tape your dad made of your piano recital. He'll think it's you practicing."

"Hmm," said Angie.

Angie really wanted to go to story hour. She and Jack set up the tape player. Then, as quietly as they could, they sneaked out of the house.

Angie and Jack went to Melden's house. "All set for story hour?" Angie asked.

Melden shook his head. "I can't go today," he said. "My parents want me to paint the shutters."

"Can't your brothers paint them for you?" asked Jack.

"I can paint! I can paint!" cried one brother.

"So can I! So can I!" screeched the other.

"Hmm," said Melden.

Melden really wanted to go to story hour.
He decided to let his brothers paint the shutters.
"Do a good job," he called as he walked off with
his friends.

Jack, Angie, and Melden headed over to the library,
where story hour was about to begin.

STORY HOUR
TODAY!

10 AM

The first story was about a boy who went to the bakery to pick up the cake his mother had ordered for his little sister's birthday. On the way home, he got hungry. "Tom peeked into the box," read the storyteller. "The cake was chocolate! His favorite! He took a tiny taste. But now the cake looked uneven, so he took a taste from the other side, and then another. Pretty soon he had eaten half the cake. Oh, no! What would his mother say?"

17

Jack wondered what *his* mother would say when she saw his room. His parents were always so proud of him when he cleaned up. His mother kissed him and said, "Good boy," and his father scratched him behind the ears. Jack did not think that would happen today.

Melden, too, was wondering about what was happening at home. His parents had trusted *him* to paint the shutters. He could imagine only too well what the house would look like when his brothers were done.

Angie was remembering her piano recital. Her dad had been so proud of her that night, and he'd gone to a lot of trouble to tape her performance. But how proud of her would he be today, when he found out she wasn't really practicing?

As the story ended, Jack stood up. "May I be excused?" he asked.

"But story hour isn't over yet," the storyteller told him.

"I know," said Jack, "but I just thought of something I have to do."

"And I have to help him," said Angie.

"Me, too," said Melden.

"We'll be right back," Jack promised, and the three friends hurried out of the library.

First they went to Melden's house. Luckily,
his brothers had painted each other instead
of the shutters.

Then they went to Angie's house, so she could finish practicing. Jack and Melden enjoyed the music. So did Angie's dad.

Finally, they went to Jack's house and cleaned his room.

They felt very proud of themselves. But now that all the painting and practicing and picking up was done, it was too late to go back to story hour.

So they had one of their own!

31